Nathaniel Eckstrom

Connected

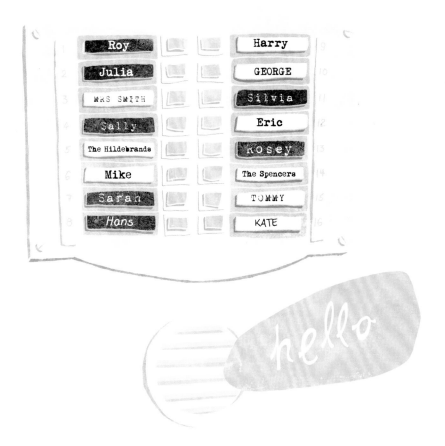

JoJo
PUBLISHING

Kate's apartment is up top, high above the city.

She can hear Tommy's singing.

Oh my, it's not pretty!

The Spencers turn up their strange music to dance.

Distracting curious Rosey, while she waters her plants.

Splish

Splash

Splish

All that downpour,

   now Eric's fish bowl is overflowing.

And why won't Sylvia's new hairdryer

stop blowing

and blowing?

That's because George, the magician, is quite good.

Oh Harry wake up!

You should see this, you should!

Hans' piano accordion sounds all through the building.

It's too much for Sarah, her ears need some shielding!

Mike isn't home much, he always works late.

shhhhhhh

The Hildebrand sisters think air mail is great!

Their best friend Sally

likes to catch her replies.

That sweet smell means Mrs Smith

is baking one of her great pies.

Julia says Mrs Smith's pies have,

"THE BEST TASTE EVER!"

Handyman Roy fixes everything. He's oh so clever!

Through all of their senses,
that's how they're *Connected*.

We're all a lot closer than
you probably expected.

for Jude

Written and illustrated by Nathaniel Eckstrom

Published by Classic Author and Publishing Services Pty Ltd

'Yarra's Edge'
2203/80 Lorimer Street
Docklands VIC 3008
Australia

Email: jo-media@bigpond.net.au
or visit www.classic-jojo.com

First Published 2014

2014 JoJo Publishing Imprint

National Library of Australia
Cataloguing-in-Publication data

Eckstrom, Nathaniel, author, illustrator.
Connected / written and illustrated by Nathaniel Eckstrom.
9780987609526 (hardback)
9780987609519 (paperback)
For primary school age.
Apartment dwellers—Fiction.
Apartment houses—Fiction.
A823.4

Edited by Riima Daher
Printed in China by Ink Asia